Other Oxford books
by Val Biro

Hungarian Folk-tales

The Magic Doctor

Jack and the Robbers
(text by Jill Bennett)

The Hobyahs

The Pied Piper of Hamelin

The Donkey that Sneezed

The Odd Job Man and the Thousand Mile Boots
(text by Jean Kenward)

Jack and the Beanstalk

The Three Little Pigs

What's up the Coconut Tree?
(text by A. H. Benjamin)

The Three Billy-Goats Gruff

The Show-Off Mouse
(text by A. H. Benjamin)

Lazy Jack

Oxford University Press, Walton Street, Oxford OX2 6DP

Oxford New York
Athens Auckland Bangkok Bogota Bombay
Buenos Aires Calcutta Cape Town Dar es Salaam
Delhi Florence Hong Kong Istanbul Karachi
Kuala Lumpur Madras Madrid Melbourne
Mexico City Nairobi Paris Singapore
Taipei Tokyo Toronto

and associated companies in
Berlin Ibadan

Oxford is a trade mark of Oxford University Press

Copyright © Val Biro 1997
First published 1997

A CIP catalogue record for this book is available
from the British Library

ISBN 0 19 279997 5 (hardback)
ISBN 0 19 272300 6 (paperback)

Printed in Hong Kong

Hansel
and
Gretel

Retold and illustrated by
Val Biro

Oxford University Press

ONCE there were two children called Hansel and Gretel. They lived with their father, who loved them dearly, and their stepmother, who did not. The family was so poor that there was not enough food to go round.

One night the stepmother said, 'We must leave the children
deep in the forest so we can have the food for ourselves.'

The children overheard
this and Hansel crept out
of the back door.

He filled his pockets
with white pebbles, then
crept back into bed.

Next morning the stepmother said, 'Children, we are going into the forest to chop wood.' She set out and they all followed her on the forest path.

As they walked along, Hansel secretly dropped the white pebbles out of his pocket, one by one.

In the middle of the great
forest the stepmother said,
'Now then, children, you wait
here until we come back.'

But they did not come back. By night time Gretel
began to cry. 'Come on,' said Hansel, 'the pebbles
will show us the way home.'

Hansel and Gretel followed
the white pebbles that glinted
in the moonlight.

They reached home by
dawn and their father
hugged them joyfully.

One night, not long afterwards, the stepmother said, 'There's only half a loaf of bread left. This time we must take the children so far into the forest that they won't be able to find their way back again.'

When Hansel overheard this, he tried to creep out for more pebbles, but now the door was locked.

Next morning the stepmother gave
the children some bread and she led
them all into the forest, but on a
different path. Hansel walked behind,
and as he had no pebbles this time he
dropped breadcrumbs instead.

When they reached the
deepest part of the forest, the
children were again told to
wait. They waited all day, and
when it was night they tried
to follow the breadcrumbs
home. But there were none
left – not a crumb.

The birds of the forest had eaten every one.

Hansel and Gretel walked all
night in the dark forest, but
they did not know which
way to turn. And by now
they were very hungry.
	Then, in the morning,
they came to a clearing.

In the middle of the clearing stood a house: a house made entirely of bread and cake and chocolate, of buns and pies and gingerbread. The roof was tiled with biscuits and the chimney was a twist of barleysugar.

The children were so hungry that they ran to the gingerbread house and broke some pieces off to eat.

Just then the door opened and a wrinkly old woman appeared.

'Well, well, dear children,' she smiled, 'you must be hungry. Come in, come in!'

Now, the old woman was really a witch – a Wicked Witch. She had built her gingerbread house to entice children in, and when they were in she would cook them and eat them up.

But now she pretended to be kind and gave Hansel and Gretel a fine dinner.

When morning came,
however, the Wicked Witch
set Gretel to work, and shut
Hansel in a cage. 'We must
fatten you up!' she cackled,
and cooked another meal
for him.

Day after day the Wicked Witch cooked a big meal for Hansel, and every night she said, 'Stretch out your finger so that I can feel how fat you're getting.'

Hansel knew that the witch had very bad sight, so he held out a bone instead.

After a month of this the Wicked Witch lost all patience. She ordered Gretel to light the oven.

'Fat or thin, I'll cook Hansel this morning!'

When the fire was blazing, the witch said, 'Now then, Gretel, just put your head in the oven to see how hot it is.'

The witch was going to cook her too, but Gretel had an idea of her own.

'I don't know how to do it,' she pretended.

'You stupid girl,' screeched
the witch. 'It's easy. Look!'
And she put her own head
in the oven. 'Like this!'

'No, like *this*!' shouted
Gretel and she pushed the
Wicked Witch right into
the oven and slammed the
door shut.

Then Gretel let Hansel out of the cage and they hugged each other. And when they found a chest in the gingerbread house filled with gold and precious stones, they crammed their pockets and ran out of the door.

Hansel and Gretel walked for hours in the
deep forest, and by the time it got dark they
realized that now they were really lost.
    Just then the moon came out and Gretel
whispered, 'Look!'

Hansel looked, and he saw a pebble.
A white pebble glinting in the
moonlight! And a little way ahead
was another – and another.

'We've found the path!' he cried with joy, and, hand in
hand, Hansel and Gretel ran all the way home.

Their father hugged and kissed them in delight.
Now that the stepmother was dead, they would live
together in peace and happiness.

And when the children showed him the precious
stones, he laughed and said, 'These are even better
than white pebbles!'